Falling for Rapunzel

PUFFIN

Falling
for
Rapunzel

Leah Wilcox

illustrated by
Lydia Monks

Once upon a bad hair day,
a prince rode up Rapunzel's way.

From up above he heard her whine,
upset her hair had lost its shine.

He thought her crying was a plea
and sallied forth to set her free.

Alas, she was too far away
to quite make out what he would say:

"Rapunzel, Rapunzel, throw down your hair!"

She thought he said,
"Your underwear".

"No, Rapunzel.
Your curly locks!"

Rapunzel threw down dirty socks.

"Please, love, just your **silky tresses!**"
She thought he asked for silky dresses.

In lace and frills up to his head,
the prince's cheeks were blushing red.

"Rapunzel, do you have a **rope?**"

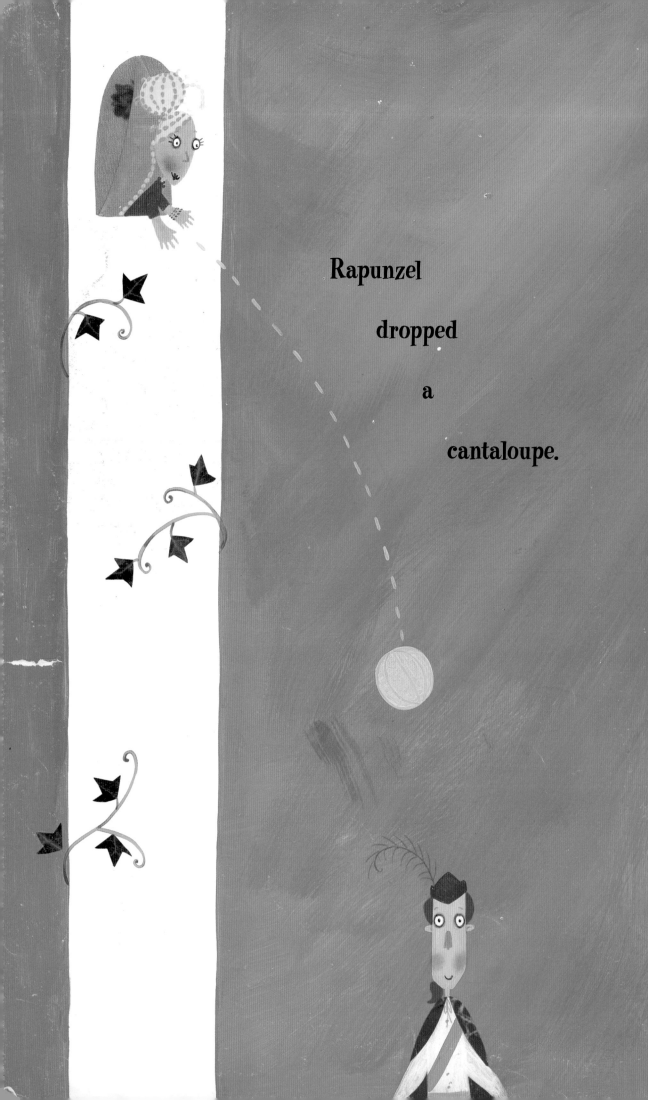

Rapunzel

dropped

a

cantaloupe.

It burst in pieces
on his head.
"Oh, bad catch!"
Rapunzel said.

"Perhaps," he sighed,
"this is a test."
And bound by love
he did not rest.

"O.K., Rapunzel, how 'bout **twine?**"

She

heaved

out

her

blue-ribbon

swine.

By now the prince was feeling hammered,
not to mention less enamoured.

He growled up, **"Do you have a ladder?"**

Rapunzel

tossed

out

pancake

batter.

It covered him from head to toe.
She yelled, "It's better cooked, you know."

At this the poor prince had a cry,
then cupped his hands for one last try:

"Rapunzel, Rapunzel,
let down your BRAID!"

Confused

Rapunzel

pushed

out

her

maid.

The maid fell squarely on the prince,
quite pleased with the coincidence.

She nimbly jumped up off his lap
and soon revived the flattened chap.

Then smiling said, "For what it's worth,
    you'll find I'm really down to earth."

His young heart thrilled, he gave a hoot,
    for what was more, the maid was cute!

She set the prince upon his steed,
then leapt behind with graceful speed.

And leaning close so he could hear,
she whispered something in his ear:

"I fell for you when we first met."
He nodded. "How could I forget?"

Rapunzel watched them ride from sight.
"I'm glad I finally heard him right!"

"I hope if they come back for more,
they'll think to knock on my back door."

For my own Prince Charming, who didn't give up on the first try.
With special thanks to Janice Graham and Rick Walton.   —L.W.

To Susan, Cecilia, Hilary and Frazer for all their support.   —L.M.

PUFFIN BOOKS

Published by the Penguin Group: London, New York, Ireland, Australia, Canada, India, New Zealand and South Africa
Penguin Books Ltd, Registered Offices: 80 Strand, London WC2R ORL, England

www.penguin.com

First published in the United States by G.P. Putnam's Sons, a division of Penguin Young Readers Group, 2003
Published in Great Britain in Puffin Books 2006
1 3 5 7 9 10 8 6 4 2
Text copyright © Leah Wilcox, 2003
Illustrations copyright © Lydia Monks, 2003
All rights reserved
The moral right of the author and illustrator has been asserted
Manufactured in China
978-0-141-50079-9
0-141-50079-4